Scruffy Goes to the Vet

Written by
Stephen Rickard

This is Scruffy.

He is my pet cat.

He likes to play with Sparks.

Sparks is our pet dog.

Scruffy is not well.

He hurt his paw when he was playing in the garden.

Now we must take him to the vet.

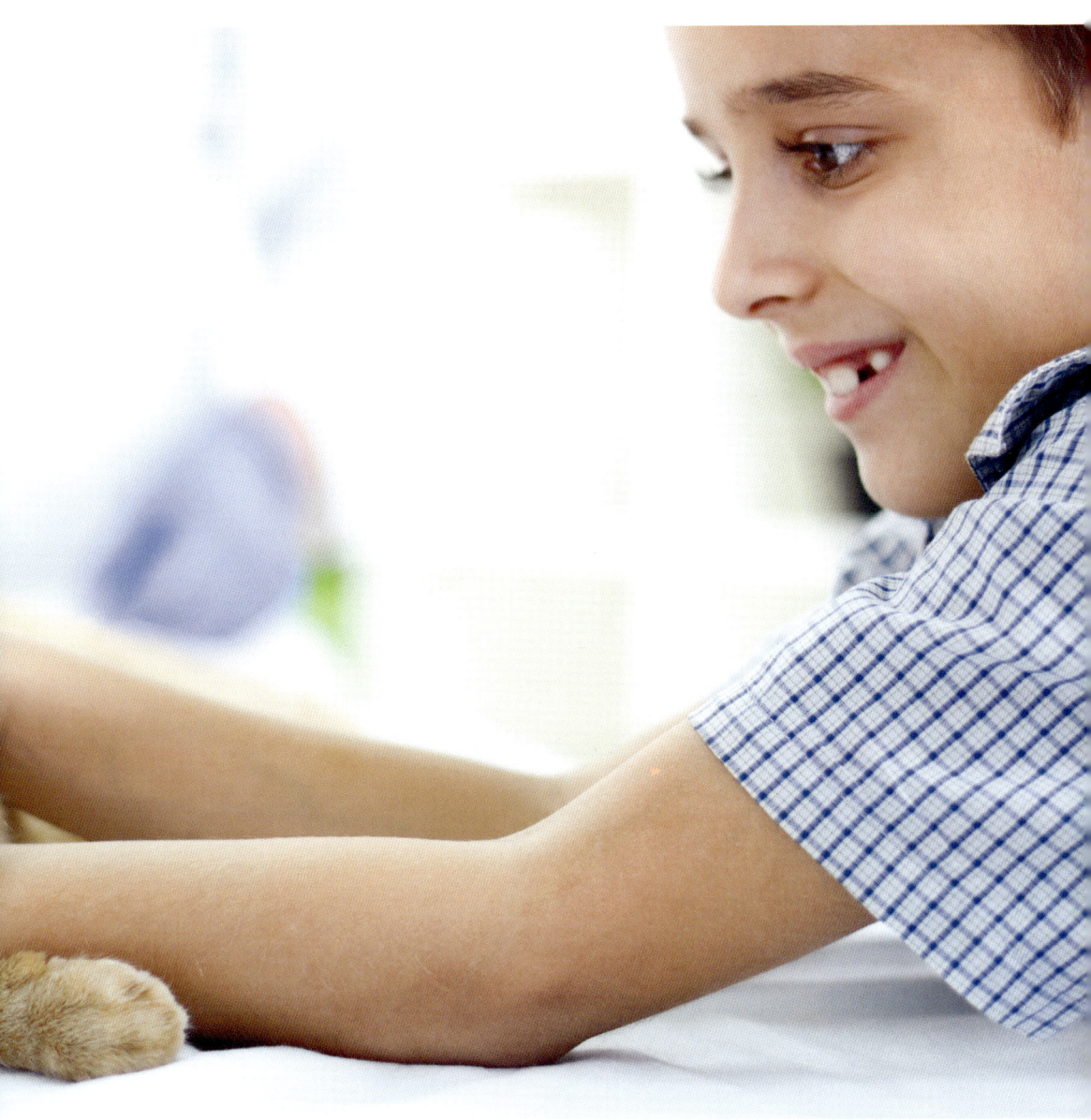

First we put Scruffy in his cage.
His cage will keep him safe.

Then we put him in the car.

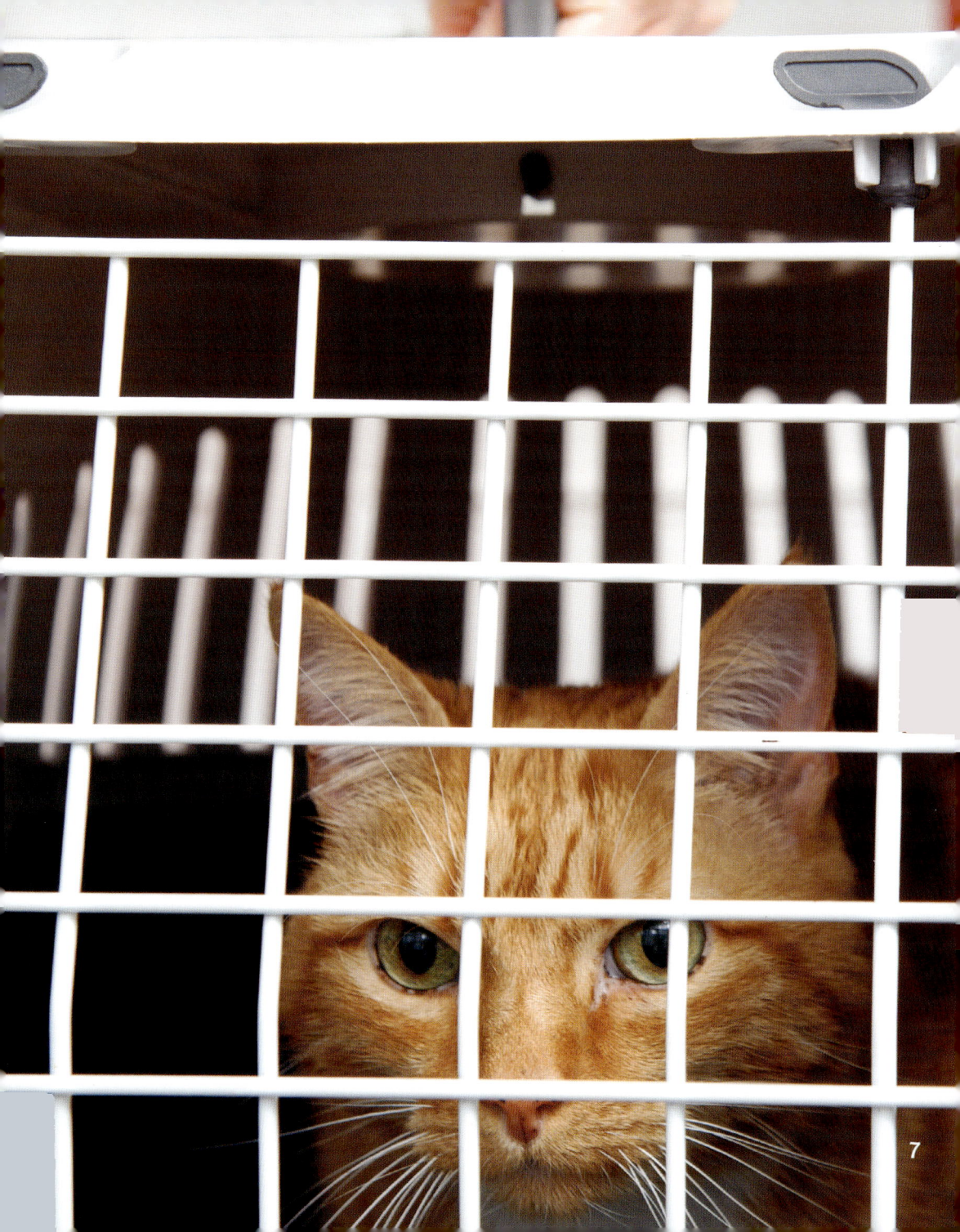

Dad drives us to the vet.

Scruffy does not like being in his cage.

At the vet we park the car and go inside.

We must wait to see the vet. Other animals are sick too.

Now it is our turn to see the vet.

He looks at Scruffy's paw. Scruffy has a nasty cut.

The vet cleans the cut. Then he puts a bandage on the paw.

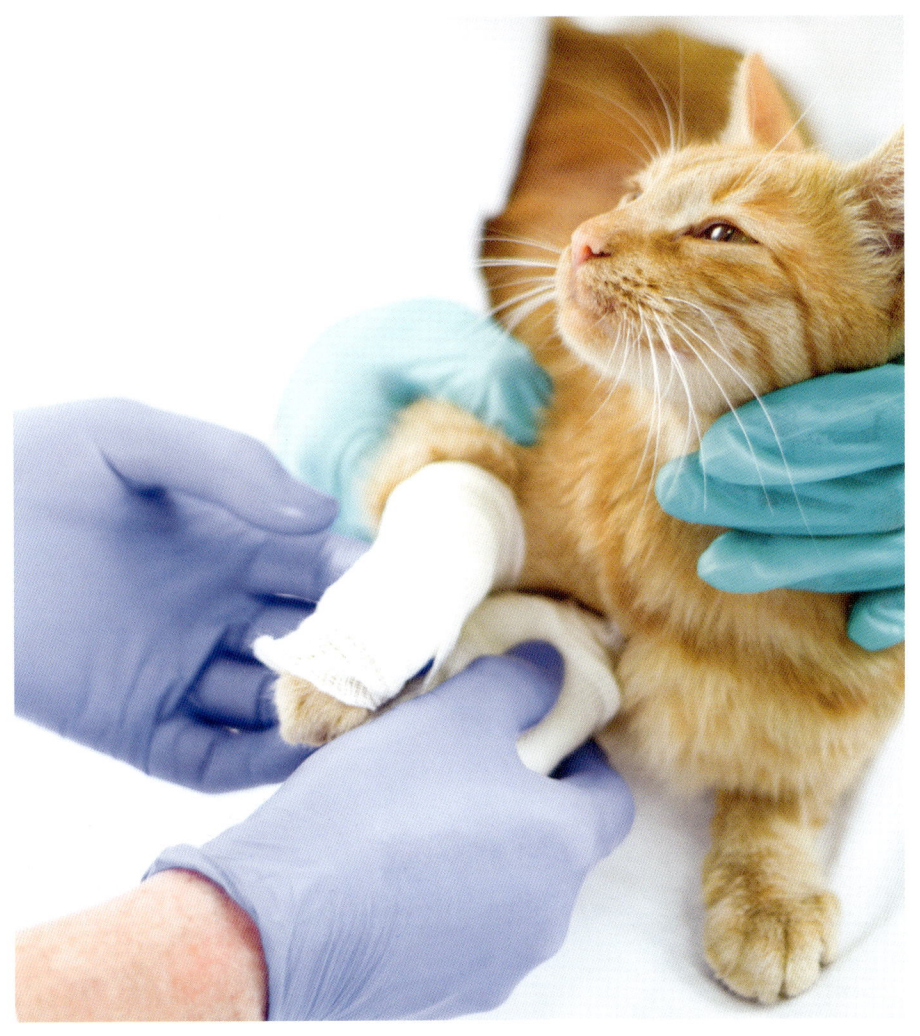

"Scruffy will be fine," the vet tells us.

"You must leave the bandage on for one week. Then bring Scruffy to see me again."

Scruffy looks very sorry for himself, but he will be well soon.

We take Scruffy back home. I am glad that his paw is not too bad.

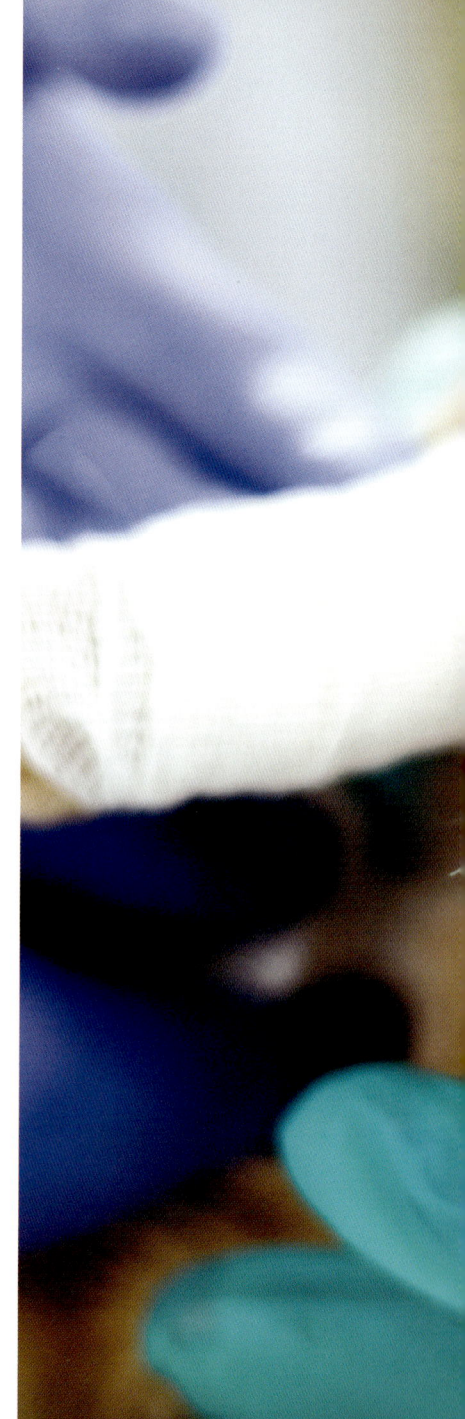

One week later, Scruffy's paw is much better. Now he can play with Sparks again.